A MOON
in my
TEACUP

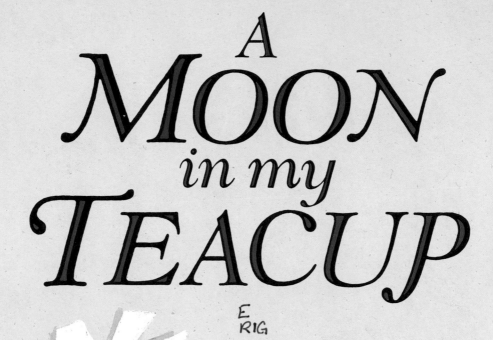

Anita Riggio

BOYDS MILLS PRESS

Copyright © 1993
by Anita Riggio
All rights reserved
Published by Caroline House
Boyds Mills Press, Inc.
A Highlights Company
815 Church Street
Honesdale, Pennsylvania 18431
Printed in Mexico

Publisher Cataloging-in-Publication Data
Riggio, Anita
    A moon in my teacup / [by] Anita Riggio : illustrations by the author.
— 1st ed.
[32]p. : col. ill. ; cm.
Summary : An eventful trip to Grandma and Grandpa's house a few days before
Christmas proves exciting and magical.
ISBN 1-56397-008-2
1. Christmas—Juvenile fiction. [1. Christmas—Fiction.] I. Title.
                [E]—dc20   1993
Library of Congress Catalog Card Number 91-77622

First edition, 1993
Book designed by Alice Lee Groton
The text of this book is set in 16-point Cochin Bold.
The illustrations are oil paintings.
Distributed by St. Martin's Press

10 9 8 7 6 5 4 3 2

For my sisters,
PATTY, MARYELLEN, and ELISSA,
who remember the moon.

And for KAREN KLOCKNER,
who believed it was there.

The narrow shingled house where Grandma, Grandpa, and the aunts live is wedged in between the Italian bakery and the shoe repair shop. My sisters and I think it looks like an old-fashioned lady breathing in to fasten her corset.

Every Sunday, it's always the same. After 12:15 Mass, we pile into the back seat of the car, and Papa drives us to Grandma and Grandpa's.

In our neighborhood, the streets are lined with houses. At this time of year Christmas wreaths hang on every door, and colored lights outline each picture window.

At Grandma and Grandpa's, the streets rumble with cars and buses and people rushing to where they are going. The tiny lights in silvery store windows blink on and off, on and off, and the bakery window is filled with sugared snowmen and coconut-sprinkled angels. *Buon Natale* is lettered on the bakery door with spray-on snow.

On the way this Sunday we sing "Deck the Halls." My big sister and I sing the words; my two little sisters are in charge of the *fa-la-las*. We all think we sound terrific.

"Any requests?" I ask Papa.

"Hmmm," he says. We wait quietly while he's thinking. "'Angels We Have Heard On High,'" Papa says finally.

"Start out softly," my big sister tells me. I nod my head.

We sing all the verses twice, and by the time we get to the last *Glo-o-o-o-ri-a,* we are singing with all our hearts. Papa parks the car and looks glad to swing the doors open just in time for *in excelsis De-o!*

Scrambling onto the sidewalk and up the steps, we stamp our boots on the porch until the snow falls off, and one of the aunts opens the door and says, "We've been waiting for you!"

We step into the house and stand for a moment blinking in the dim hallway. We can smell Grandma's special cookies. The high ceilings make us quiet.

Peeking around the corner, we see the Christmas village in the parlor. Grandpa made each house and shop himself. He made the inn and stable too. The village seems empty, but my sisters and I keep a lookout for the tiny villagers who we're sure are hiding there.

Grandpa greets us with hello kisses. Then one by one we hug Grandma, who sits smiling in her chair near the window. My little sisters reach into their pockets for the paper snowflakes they've made. *"Care piccine! Grazia,* sweet children," Grandma says, and squeezes the girls tighter.

The calendar with twenty-four tiny windows hangs in the dining room. Twenty-two windows have been opened already. There are mama sheep with their baby lambs, a cow and an ox, a village with palm trees. Angels with baby-doll faces smile out at me.

This Sunday, it's my turn to open a window: a full moon shines on a man, a woman, and a small donkey. I know the story by heart. They are looking for a place to rest, but there will be no room for them at the inn.

While Papa and Grandpa talk about salting the slate walk, we help the aunts clear the newspapers and mail off the big dining room table. The teacups and saucers are stacked next to the wreath on the credenza. My big sister lifts them down, and the little ones help her set them at each place.

In the kitchen I help stack Grandma's *biscotti* on a fancy plate. Then, walking slowly and watching my feet, I carry the cookies to the table.

One aunt pours tea.
"Milk or lemon?" she asks.

The grownups are too busy talking to notice a moon
shining in our teacups. Only my sisters and I see.

"Look!" my littlest sister whispers. "It's just like the
moon in the calendar!"

Someone taps a finger on the table, and the moon bursts
into a cupful of sparkles that twinkle and glisten and dance.
Soon the hand lies flat, and the sparkles dim.

But the moon still shimmers in our teacups like a secret, a sign.

After tea, while the grownups are talking about Christmas shopping and snowstorms, my big sister takes the little ones to the bathroom at the top of the dark, spooky stairs. I hear each step whine under their feet, even though they try to creep up without making a sound. There are other doors at the top of the stairs, and my sisters tiptoe past them quickly, before Something that might be hiding there jumps out.

In the meantime, I choose a popcorn ball wrapped in cellophane from the bowl in the pantry and wander down the hallway through the doors and into the parlor, dark and still.

I sink into the velvet chair to look
for the villagers, who went scurrying
for their shops and houses when they
heard me coming, crunching.

But this Sunday I find someone in
the stable.
There is a man, a woman, and a
small donkey.
And in the manger lies a tiny child.

"Oh," I whisper to the baby, "I know who you are. Soon angels with bright wings will come to sing for you. Then some shepherds will stop by. You'll like the little lambs they'll bring. And after the shepherds, three kings will come with birthday presents—just for you.

"I can play 'Silent Night' with two hands," I tell him. "May I play it for you?"

Very gently I lift the baby in his manger and carry him to the piano. I hope his mother won't mind. I hear murmurs from the grownups in the dining room as I climb onto the bench. I press one key, and the note rings out rich and low.

As I play, the music fills up the room and spills out the doors. I remember to sing as softly as I can. The words "heavenly peace" bump against the ceiling and then float down, silent as snowflakes.

The quiet is thick.

On tiptoe, I bring the baby back to the stable. "Happy birthday," I whisper to the tiny boy sleeping among the boughs.

At that instant, my sisters thunder down the staircase, sure they've seen Something.

"Quick! Come here!" I whisper,
but it's too late. I hear Papa's chair
scrape the floor.

"Time to go," he calls.

The aunts gather our coats from
the wide oak rack. Grandma tucks
cookies into our fists, one for each
hand. Then we're stuffed into boots
and coats, mittens and hats, and get
passed from one adult to the next
for kisses and hugs.

Not even my sisters have noticed the angels
with bright wings, the shepherds with their lambs,
and the kings with their presents come to visit the
man, the woman, the donkey, and the tiny child.

But I see them all there in the village,

like the glimmer of a moon in my teacup.